Good Night Phobos, Good Night Deimos

Written by
Tim Baird

Illustrated by
Jamie Noble Frier

This story is dedicated to all the young boys and girls out there who were born on Earth but are destined to explore beyond our planetary gravity well. May you dream tonight of new adventures out in our solar system (and beyond) and someday get ready for bed on another planet...

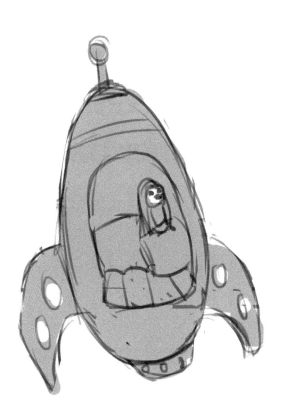

In the inflatable gray hab,
There was a communicator,
A weather balloon,
And a picture of —

A rover jumping over a dune.

**And there were three little jars
with soil from Mars.**

And two chunks of iron,
And a model of Saturn.

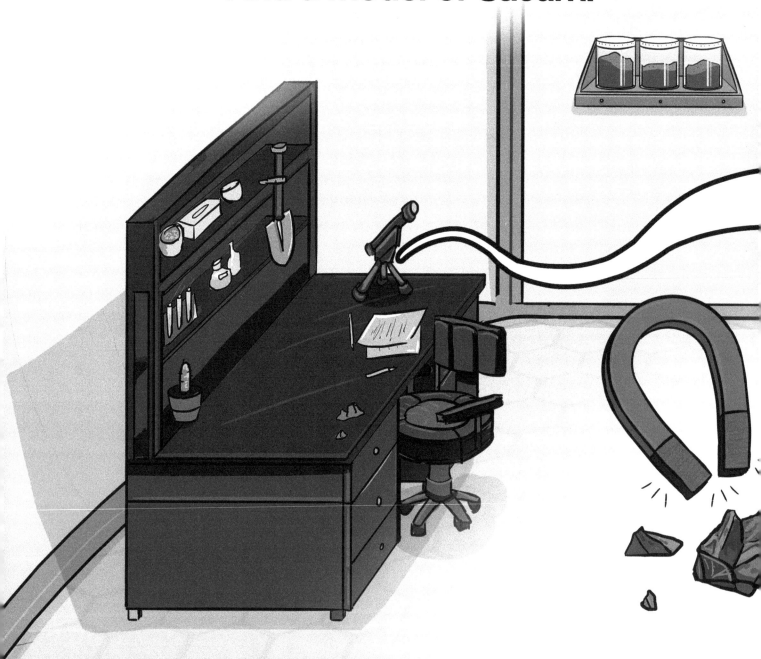

And a little tardigrade,
And a gently used spade.

And a desk, and a seat, and some rehydrated meat.

And a stubborn old astronaut
who still measures in 'feet'.

Good night, hab.

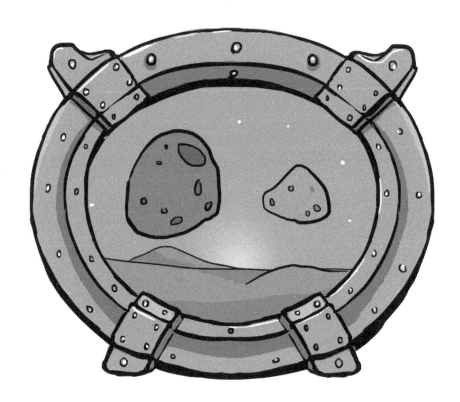

**Good night Phobos,
Good night Deimos.**

**Good night rover
jumping over a dune.**

Good night lamp.
And the weather balloon.
Good night jars.
Good night Mars.

Good night iron.

And good night Saturn.

Good night sprocket,
And good night rocket.

Good night little tardigrade.

And good night spade.

Good night desk.

And good night seat.

Good night airlock.

Good night meat.

And good night to the astronaut who still measures in 'feet'.

Good night carbon dioxide.

Good night Mars.

Good night astronauts sleeping amongst the stars.

Acknowledgements

Tim Baird

As always, none of this could be possible without the love and support of my family: Kristin and Liam. You have believed in me from Day One and cheered me on each step of the way. Thank you.

Thank you to Jamie Noble Frier for taking my crazy collection of poorly drawn hand sketches and turning them into a real work of art. You have a wonderful way of interpreting people's ideas and crafting a fun, light-hearted illustrated world for the reader to dive into and explore. Thanks for putting up with me throughout this journey and helping me to craft my first children's book.

Lastly, thank you to the enthusiastic team of beta readers, especially Jackie, Jake, Jeff, Jennifer, Michael, Sarah, Stephen, and Tracy, who shared my initial concept sketches and words with their families to test out the draft manuscript. Your feedback, from both kids and adults, helped to shape this book into its final form which you're reading today.

Jamie Noble Frier

Thanks to Tim who has been a pleasure to work alongside with his great imagination and infectious passion for the story and illustrations.

Thanks to my wife for making reading a staple of our children's day. Thanks to my children with whom I get to join in adventures in every book we read together.

Thanks to those who supported me when I said I wanted to stop serving pizzas and start drawing aliens and dragons instead. I know it seemed like a bold move at the time.

About the Author

Tim Baird spends his days lost in the world of medical device design and manufacturing. Volunteering with children in several youth robotics programs, he is trying his hardest to avoid growing up, one robot at a time. When he's not designing or writing, he enjoys time at home with his wife & son, watching/reading anything Star Wars related, and spending time out in the woods of New England. Other works by Tim Baird include the YA fantasy series, *The Dragon in the Whites*, and the SF novella, *Eggs in Two Baskets*.

About the Illustrator

Jamie Noble Frier is a freelance digital artist from Sussex, UK. He primarily takes on contracts in fiction literature cover design/illustration, board game projects, video games, and corporate illustration and graphic design.

Among many others, Jamie has provided artwork for League of Legends (Riot Games), Magicka (board game licensed by Paradox Interactive), Ed Greenwood (Forgotten Realms, Dungeons and Dragons) and Richard A Knaak (author of Warcraft, Dragonlance and Diablo series of books). Find Jamie at www.TheNobleArtist.com

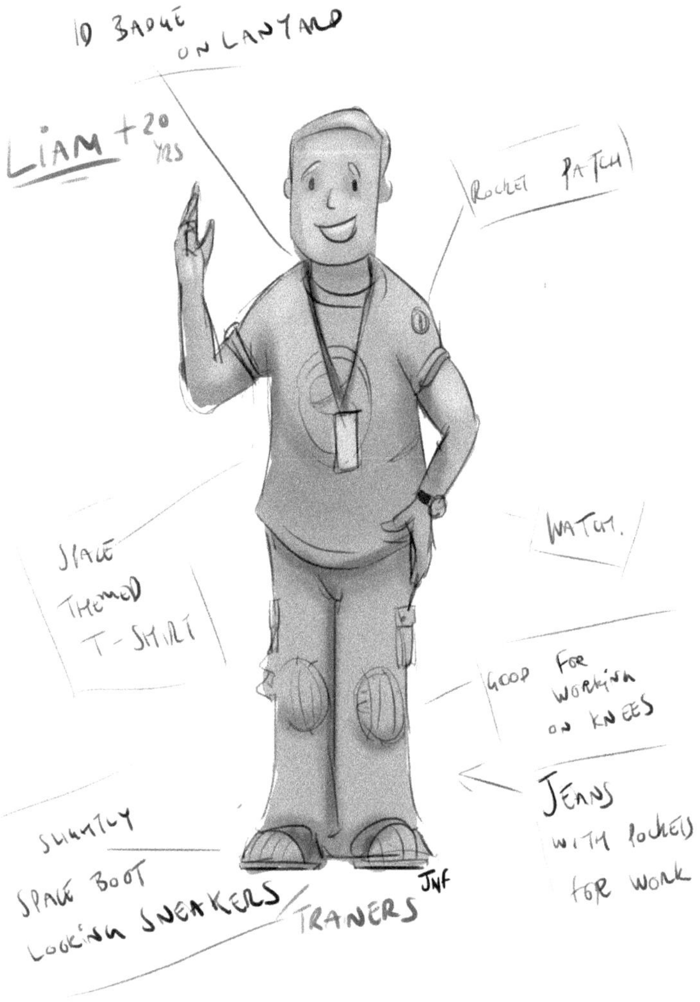
ID BADGE ON LANYARD
LIAM + 20 YRS
ROCKET PATCH
SPACE THEMED T-SHIRT
WATCH.
GOOD FOR WORKING ON KNEES
JEANS WITH POCKETS FOR WORK
SLIGHTLY SPACE BOOT LOOKING SNEAKERS / TRANERS
JNF

CPSIA information can be obtained
at www.ICGtesting.com
Printed in the USA
LVHW071231220721
693407LV00005B/97